"I was born in London in 1946 and grew up in a sweet shop in Essex. For several years I worked as a graphic designer, but in 1980 I decided to concentrate on writing and illustrating books for children.

My wife, Annette, and I have two grown-up children, Ben and Amanda, and we have put down roots in Suffolk.

I haven't recently counted how many books there are with my name on the cover but Percy the Park Keeper accounts for a good many of them. I'm reliably informed that they have sold more than three million copies. Hooray!

I didn't realise this when I invented Percy, but I can now see that he's very like my mum's dad, my grandpa. I even have a picture of him giving a ride to my brother and me in his old home-made wooden wheelbarrow!"

NICK BUTTERWORTH

PERCY'S FRIENDS
THE SQUIRRELS

NICK BUTTERWORTH

Collins

An imprint of HarperCollinsPublishers

Thanks Graham Daldry. You're a wizard.

Thanks Atholl McDonald. You're a hero!

First published in Great Britain by HarperCollins Publishers Ltd in 2002

1 3 5 7 9 10 8 6 4 2

ISBN: 0 00 711980 1

Text and illustrations copyright © Nick Butterworth 2002
The author asserts the moral right to be identified as the author of the work.

The HarperCollins website address is: www.**fire**and**water**.com

Printed and bound in Belgium

MY FRIENDS
THE SQUIRRELS

Squirrels are bright and quick thinking. They move quickly too and not just over the ground. They seem to be able to whizz straight up a tree as if it were a fallen log!

They like to explore, which can get them into trouble sometimes. I remember an awful kerfuffle once, when a squirrel got stuck in a rabbit hole. Unlike the mole, squirrels are not good at going backwards. I believe it's something to do with bushy tails.

Squirrels can be very forgetful. They never, never seem to remember where they have stored their food. Which reminds me, I put a sandwich down a moment ago. You haven't seen it, have you?

Once, when I was on my way to pick some apples, I noticed three squirrels up in the branches of an oak tree, collecting acorns. I thought how nice it would be, if I could pick my apples like that.

Suddenly, I had a brainwave. My apples could be picked in exactly the same way!

Now, in the autumn, the squirrels help to pick all those apples that are so hard to get at the tops of the trees. And I pick the easy ones that I can reach without having to use my ladder.

It's a very good arrangement. It is strange though. I've noticed a lot more apples have little teeth marks in them than when I used to pick them by myself.

SQUIRRELS REALLY LIKE . . .

Balancing. They seem to be able to balance
on just about anything, although there have
been one or two accidents on my washing line!

Nuts. Not just acorns and beech nuts. They like
peanuts, coconut and hazelnuts too. And they
don't mind if they're covered in chocolate!

SQUIRRELS DON'T LIKE ...

Lightning. I love to watch it myself,
but I suppose it's different if you live at
the top of a tall tree!

Being underground.
Here are two squirrels with their friend,
the mole. Guess which is which!

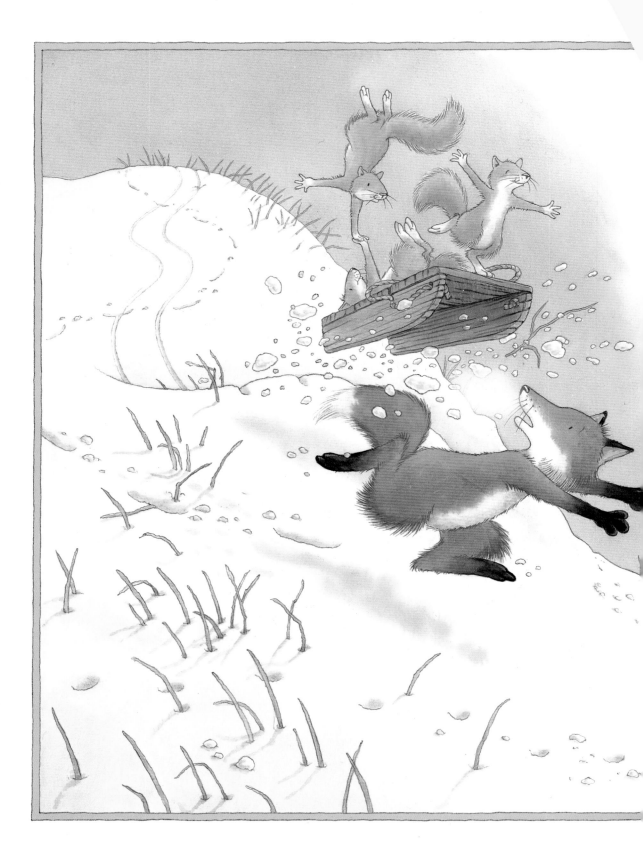

Everybody loves tobogganing! Well, nearly everybody. Actually, I don't think the owl likes it all that much. And I don't think my Auntie Joyce is too keen . . . But I think just about everyone else loves tobogganing.

The squirrels are especially good at it. Some of their high-speed acrobatics are just amazing.

I think the squirrels would agree though, that their steering of a toboggan is not quite so amazing.

In fact, sometimes, it's not at all amazing.

It's amusing.

I've got lots of pictures in my photo album.

This palm tree
is made from
flower pots
and fern leaves.
The two little
monkeys are
made from
squirrels!

The little
monkeys
broke my
flower
pots!

Here are some I took of my good friends, the squirrels.

Squirrels do stop for a rest sometimes. These four were caught napping in my potting shed.

My old wheelbarrow makes a perfect exercise wheel!

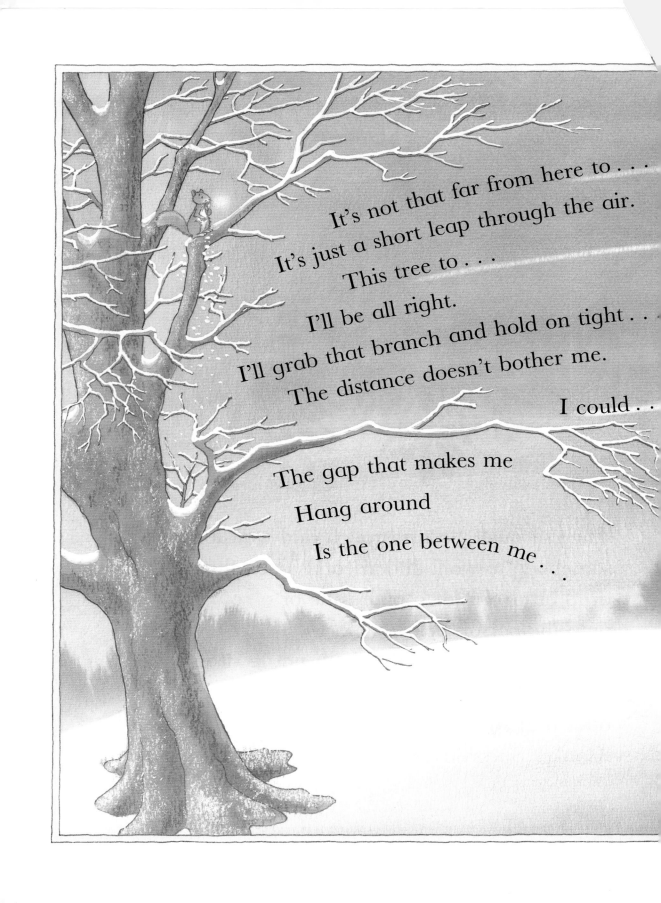

It's not that far from here to . . .
It's just a short leap through the air.
This tree to . . .
I'll be all right.
I'll grab that branch and hold on tight . . .
The distance doesn't bother me.

I could . . .

The gap that makes me

Hang around

Is the one between me . . .

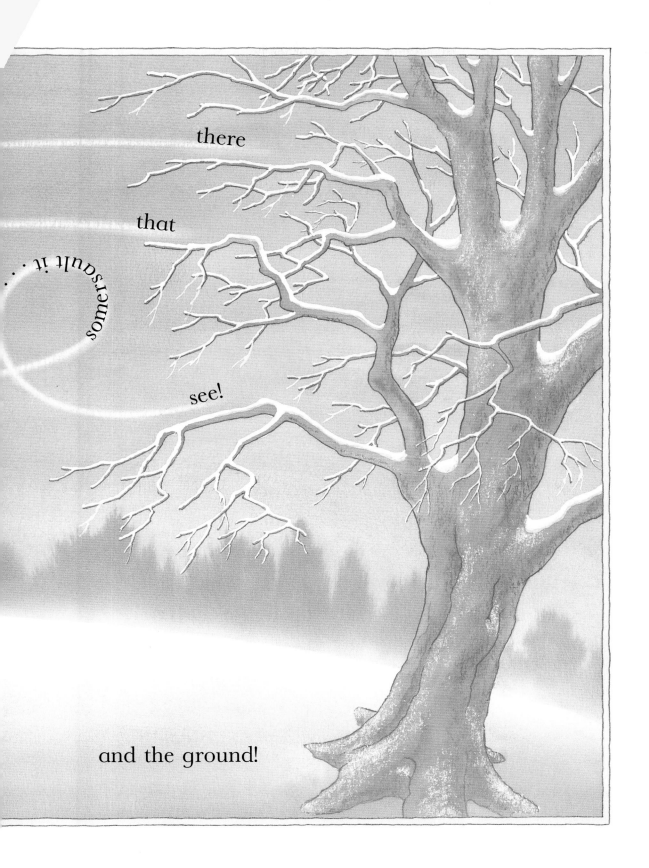

there

that

somersault it . . .

see!

and the ground!

FAVOURITE PLACES

The squirrels seem to have quite a few favourite places. One that I can think of is a small clearing in the middle of the pine wood which they call the Mushroom Field. They call it that because of the lovely big mushrooms that grow there.

On a misty, autumn morning, if you get up early enough, that's where you'll find the squirrels, having a very tasty breakfast!

Now, if I asked what you would expect to find waving in the breeze at the top of a flag pole, the sensible answer would be a flag. You probably wouldn't say squirrels! Not unless you have been to *this* park.

But if you have, you might have seen some of my squirrel friends enjoying the view from another of their favourite places. They tell me there is just enough room for three. Four is a bit of a squash.

I say, there doesn't look to be room even for one! I tell them to be very careful. I suggest that they might be just a little safer leaping through the branches of the big oak tree house which, of course, is where they live.

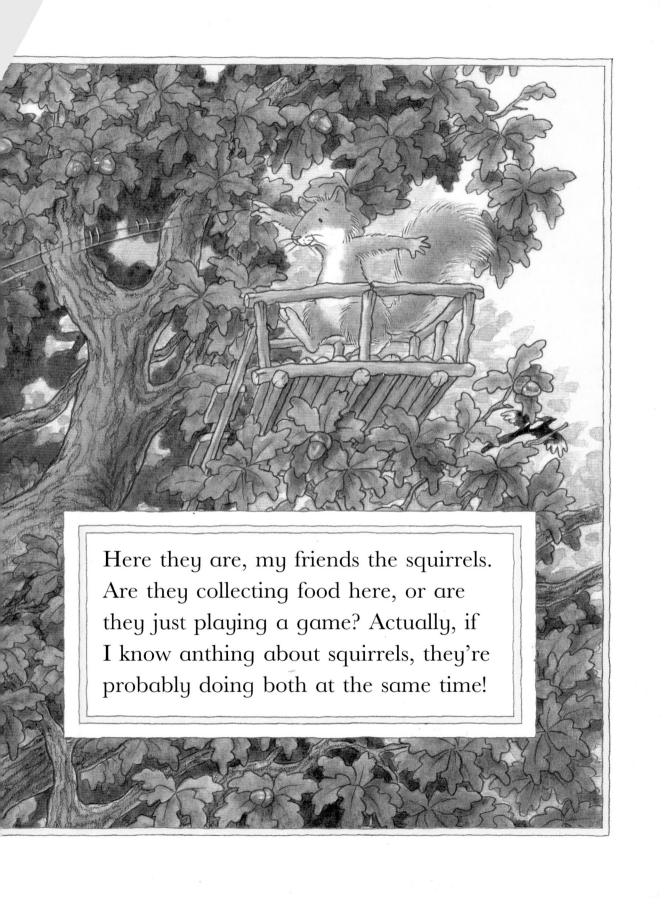

Here they are, my friends the squirrels.
Are they collecting food here, or are
they just playing a game? Actually, if
I know anthing about squirrels, they're
probably doing both at the same time!

Poster not shown to size. Actual size: 120cms x 80cms

THE TREE HOUSE

In this picture you'll see Percy the Park Keeper and his friends. But if you look very carefully, you can also find a balloon, a kite, a hot-water bottle, a model aeroplane, a paintbrush, a robin, a beach ball, a magpie, a yo-yo, Percy's stripy mug, a pencil, a conker, Percy's watering can, a cheese roll, a framed picture of Percy, one of Percy's gardening gloves, a model yacht, a plastic duck, a banana, and a frog. Oh, and ten ladybirds!

FREE GIANT POSTER

Nick Butterworth's new, giant picture of the tree house
in Percy's Park shows Percy and all his animal friends
in and around their tree house home. There are also
lots of things hidden in the picture. Some are easy
to find. Some are much harder!

To send off for your free poster, simply snip off
FOUR tokens, each from a different book in the
Percy the Park Keeper and his Friends series and send them
to the address below. Remember to include
your name, address and age.

Percy Poster, Children's Marketing Department,
HarperCollins Publishers, 77-85 Fulham Palace Road, London W6 8JB

Offer applies to UK and Eire only. Available while stocks last.
Allow 28 days for delivery.

Read all the stories about Percy and his animal friends...

Percy toys and videos
are also available.

PERCY THE PARK KEEPER
AND HIS FRIENDS

Really get to know Percy the Park Keeper
and his friends in this exciting new series.
Find out where the animals play, the things
they like and the things they don't, and enjoy looking
at funny moments captured on camera by Percy!

There are lots of titles in the series for you to collect:

Send off for a stunning, free poster when you buy any four titles.
Percy's park has never been so much fun!

Collins

£2.99

ISBN 0-00-711980-1

00299>

9 780007 119806

PERCY'S FRIEND
THE MOLE

NICK BUTTERWORTH